THE WAR OF THE DRAGONS

Fire Dragons, Ice Dragons, and Water Dragons
All Controlled by the Powerful Dragon Sword

by

Ronald D. Goode
and
Katherine M. Camacho

Dorrance Publishing Co
585 Alpha Drive
Pittsburgh, PA 15238
Visit our website at *www.dorrancebookstore.com*

ISBN: 978-1-6386-7255-5
eISBN: 978-1-6386-7607-2

The War of the Dragons

Fire Dragons, Ice Dragons, and Water Dragons
All Controlled by the Powerful Dragon Sword

by

Ronald D. Goode
and
Katherine M. Camacho

Introduction

In the times before human inhabitants existed, God created the dragons of all species: fire dragons, whose flames melted through all matter; ice dragons, who froze all matters; water dragons' water broke all matter. The Dragon Sword had the power to control the dragons and destroy the dragons. They roamed the Earth with jinns, which were spirits made out of smoke. The dragons cause the dinosaurs to become extinct by using them as their food resource.

Once the first man was created by God, Adam, man was by his self so God created a woman from Adam's crooked rib, who became Eva. The both of them disobeyed God in heaven, so he sent them to Earth with the Dragon Sword for punishment, then spread many men and women across the world who the dragons fed on for millions of years. The dragons guarded the sword because they knew the sword was the destruction of their life and controlled them. For some time, people worshipped the dragons and made sacrifices, taking people to the caves, bound, to feed them to the dragon to keep the dragons from coming out of the cave and attacking all the pagan people. This went on for hundreds and hundreds of years unto the dragons grew in numbers and started coming out of the caves and attacking people. Still to this day people worship the dragons and have statues of dragon gods in their home.

Back in the Biblical time, dragons of all species in the hot hemispheres were eating people. Ice dragons in the cold hemisphere were eating people. Water dragons in the Victoria waterfall in Africa were eating animals in the seas. God also placed the Dragon Sword of power in the mountains of Arunachal to control the dragons. The sword possessed the power to shoot out fire, water, and ice, and could go a far distance. There were prophecies going around ever since man was created: it was going to be a boy born to bear the Dragon Sword. The boy's name was going to be Quintin. He would be the emperor over the dragons, and his bloodline would be Kings and Queens over the dragons; they would be the only ones the dragons listened to. The descendants of the emperor raged war on all pagan countries until everyone submitted to their monotheistic beliefs.

Once they conquered the world and the emperor was called back to God, the Dragon Sword went back in its rightful place: in stone. His offspring started go to war against one another to be the one to bear the sword. God cursed them for being deceptive, and none of the Emperors or Empresses were picked. Instead, one of his grandsons was to be their Chosen One to bear the sword, control of dragons, and rule over all the dragons and the people of the world.

Chapter 1
Kuru Kingdom, the City of Mountains, Arunachal

The fire dragons and the Dragon Sword were in a cave where the city people worshipped the dragons. They were the tribe of Arunachal, and the Kuru King of the tribe made sacrifices by ordering his soldiers to give the sick, weak, old, and the people who broke the laws to the dragons as an offering for sacrifice. The dragons were well fed, eating the tribespeople. The tribe lives this way for a long time and still worshipped the dragon gods.

Time passed, and people had dragon statues as gods in their home, but the pagan belief start fading away. Other worshipers were worshiping God according to the monotheistic belief in the city of Arunachal. God gave an old man visions to inform the city's people to worship God, the one true God, and he was going to send warrior-horsemen to help with the dragons. The people didn't believe him; the people worshipped the dragon gods indoors and did not want to give their dragon gods up. God kept giving the old man prophecies and chose him to be the messenger to the city of Arunachal. The people still did not take heed, so God allowed the dragons to keep attacking the city and eating the people.

The city people believed the old man was insane. The old man, named Ezra, kept giving prophecies: God was going to send warrior-horsemen from Jerusalem to help with the dragons. One of the warrior-horsemen was going to give the city a son who was going to bear the

Dragon Sword. Once all the warrior-horsemen were gone, the boy was going to be of age to go in the dragon cave and retrieve the Dragon Sword and become the emperor over the dragons and have them under his control. The emperor's kids would become Kings and Queens, then Emperors and Empresses over the dragons; only their bloodline could control the dragons and ride the dragons. All nations that were pagans were going to be ordered to be destroyed by God unless they accepted the monotheistic belief, worshipped only one God, the true God of all living things. Once they were on the path of one God of Abraham, they would be under the control of the Emperor and the dragons.

The dragons came out the cave, caught the people off guard, and scooped up five people. The people ran to the caves, knowing the dragons could not get into the cave because the entry was too little. The dragons went back to their cave. The family members of the people who were taken were weeping and could not do nothing to help them.

The old man told the people God was sending help. The monk prayed with the families who lost their loved ones. Once the dragons were gone, the people came out of the caves and attended to their land and crops.

<h1 style="text-align:center">Chapter 2</h1>

The next day, the people of the city were holding a memorial for the five people who were taken by the dragons. The Kuru King's successor, King Raja, believed the city was cursed. The last time he sent men, they were all slaughtered and eaten by the dragons. Nobody in the Kuru Kingdom traveled to the City of Mountains. Once the monks washed the bodies of the deceased, the people gathered around to pay their respect as the monks pushed the bodies to the sea, and the fire was set to them as they burned, going further into the sea.

The next day, the people were in service in the secret house. The dragon bell started to sound off, and the people start running and looking for the dragons. For once, they didn't see any dragons, they saw four horsemen in armor approach the city. They were in shock and speechless; some people were running around saying, "The knights' saviors are coming!"

Some people were saying to one another, "The old fool wasn't lying."

Some people fell to their knees, crying to God of joy in spite of the agony and suffering they'd been through, thanking God for freeing them from the suffering they'd been through their whole life. In the city, the knights' saviors came through the city entrance and gave a note to the monk saying they were there from the high, sacred house in Jerusalem in order to help them with the dragons, and they were commanded to stay until the dragon problem was under control.

The people accepted them with open arms and fed them and watered their horses from a long journey. The warrior-horsemen were giving beds in the upper part of the sacred house. Once they saw the old man, they notice him right away from the description as being God's messenger, and they greeted the messenger. He informed the warrior-horsemen that God had been giving him prophecies of them coming to save the people, and that one would give the city a son to bear the sword. They said, "Who going to be the one to marry one of the city's virgins?"

They started looking at one another, and the old man's daughter came in the church. They were amazed by her presence and beauty. She told them her name was Amira, which means princess. They introduced themselves as Abbas, meaning lion; Abid, worshipper; Ajmal, very handsome; and Amin, truthful. Amira chose Ajmal for a husband, and the both of them waited for a couple days, so they could get to know one another until they got married.

When the time came, the both of them got married in front of the whole city. The people gave them gifts and built them a small house. The city people respected Ezra as God's messenger now.

"By the Grace of God, he was showing us His mercy. He was upset with this city for many years for idol worshiping and taking the dragons as gods. We are still here doing God's work; we're going to fight side-by-side with the warrior-horsemen until the boy is born and saves the world from the dragons, and cleanses it of the idle worshipers joining partners with God," Ezra said.

Chapter 3

The dragon bell was sounding off. The kids, women, and old people went towards the mountains while Abbas, Abid, Ajmal, and Amin waited on guard. The city men were also ready with spears that could pierce the dragons' hides.

Once the dragons reached, the city flames came down on houses. As the houses disintegrated, they threw their spears. Abbas shot a harpoon, killing one of the dragons while another dragon disintegrated Abbas, killing him instantly. Amin had the strength of five men and shot an arrow the size of a spear out a bow and arrow at the dragon. The dragon flames were coming down on him, and Amin disintegrated into ashes, but the arrow went through the dragon, killing him. The dragon hit the ground, putting a crater in the ground, and some men started to get scared of the flames and tried to run to the mountains. Another dragon scooped them up and went flying back towards the caves.

The people came out of the cave once the dragons were gone and start cheering once they saw the dragons die for the first time in history. The people got scooped up, their love ones were looking for them. Once they knew the dragons got hold of them, they dropped to their knees and started praying to God to let their loved ones into heaven.

The dragons were now in hibernation. The city people built their houses back up, and Ajmal and Abid built tunnels to move underground to throw the dragons off and be able to sneak attack them. Arima gave birth to a baby boy. She named him Quinton, the savior.

The sky lit up, and the dragons woke up from hibernation. The people witnessed the sky light up, and they believed the boy was the savior and could retrieve the sword and control the dragons. They placed gifts at Arima's house for the baby. Quinton was being protected by the angels, and the dragons could not see Quinton, nor anybody next to him. Erza informed the city that everybody must follow the monks. The people still had the dragons gods in their houses, which upset God. The people went and got their statues and burned them. The whole city was following the monks' monotheistic beliefs.

Everybody's home led to the tunnels, and the tunnels had many exits to the caves in the mountains. The people did not have to run into the open to get to the tunnels. Time passed, and the dragons were out of hibernation. The people got food in the tunnels. The day was a busy day in the city. The dragon bell sounded off, and some people went under the tunnel while the rest of the people made it to the caves. The dragons didn't see anyone in sight, so they took some of the animals and went back to the caves. The people came out the caves and went back to their daily lives. People were talking about how life was better for them with the savior there giving them hope to fight for a better future. The people learned how to make weapons to kill the dragons and hurt them to keep them away.

Years passed by, and Ajmal taught his son Quinton how to use a sword and ride horses. The dragons attacked many times, killing people and animals, but the people fought the dragons and out slicked the dragons to stay alive. The messenger Ezra lost his sight due to sickness, and his daughter, Arima, was taking care of him and guided him where he needed to go. Quinton was at the age to bear the sword.

The dragon bell went off, and Abid and Ajmal were waiting with the harpoons to kill the dragons. The dragons' flames were burning through the dirt on the ground, destroying one of the tunnels and killing people. Abid and Ajmal sent four harpoons into the air, knocking two dragons out of the air, wounding them badly. They were bleeding out. Abid and Ajmal threw two more harpoons, but the dragon went around the harpoon and killed Abid with flames, burning his skin off his body. Ajmal hit the dragon in the heart, causing the dragon to crash in front of him. The force threw him back so far, he broke all the bones in his body, causing him to die slowly in his wife's arms.

Quinton was with his mother attending to his father. Once the dragons saw Quinton, they retreated back to the caves, leaving the death total in the city at the highest it had ever been. Ajmal told his wife that the time had come; he was going with God.

"Quinton, it's time for you to retrieve the sword and take control of all the dragons and drive paganism out of God's lands," Ajmal told his son.

Quinton told his father, "Do not die, I need you."

His father said he was going to be in a better place, and they would see each other again in heaven, adding, "God chose you. You must do what you were chosen for. You are protected by the angels, so no harm can touch you."

His son hugged him.

Ajmal slowly slipped away towards death. The city people started losing hope after Abid and Ajmal's death. Abid and Ajmal gave them hope by showing them how to defend themselves and fought for them for a long time.

CHAPTER 4

The next day, the city people gave their loves ones barbarian burials by placing their love ones on wood coffins in the water and pushing them to the sea, sending arrows of fire to burn their bodies. Bodies were spreading out to the sea. The day of the attack, 50 people were killed.

The rituals were done with the dead. Quinton left the people and went towards the caves where the dragons lived. The people watched him as he approached the cave's entrance, which was the size of a giant. Quinton went in the cave and immediately he sensed the sword. He was born with the sense to find the sword wherever it was, and he was the only one who could bear the sword. Quinton walked and walked until he came face-to-face with the dragons. They were sleeping when he walked by the dragons. They opened their eyes up a little bit to peek, but they couldn't see Quinton because the angels were covering him. Quinton reached the sword, and the sword lit up. Quinton pulled the sword out of the huge rock, and the dragons' eyes opened up wide. Angel Gabriel covered Quinton and the sword, so he could pass by the dragons.

Once Quinton got to the entrance, the angels uncovered him. The dragons were coming. Quinton ran down the mountain until he reached the city. The people were scared, happy, and at a loss for words when they saw the sword in Quinton's hand. The dragons came out of the cave, and the Angel Gabriel told Quinton, "Once the dragons reach the city, just point the sword at them, and they will obey and submit. If the dragons rebel, just tell the sword to shoot out what you want to come out: fire, water, ice, or make it go the distance to cut them out of the air."

The dragons reached the city. Quinton talked to the dragons in dragon tongue, telling them to submit to him. The dragons looked at him and at one another, wondering how Quinton could talk to them. Quinton pointed the sword at the dragons; all of them but two submitted. Quinton froze the first dragon, and the second dragon tried to burn him, so Quinton send flames to the dragon, causing him to burn up. Quinton then cut the dragon in half. The dragons bowed down to him; the city people followed after seeing what took place. Quinton started talking to the dragons.

"I am chosen by God. He created dragons to test all His species. Dragons are ordered by me having the sword to submit. Follow me, and drive pagans out of God's lands and only have mercy on the people who submit and worship the one true God of Abraham. The people who turn on their heels and worship any other than the one true God, we are ordered by God to make judgment, and we will sentence them to burn. We are under the control of the sword. God entrusted me with this. I am the Dragon Emperor. We follow the sword and respect the sword."

The people bowed down, and the Dragon's followed. Quinton said, "This is the Holy City of Arunachal, the land of mountains. The Kuru Dynasty abandoned these lands. God is by our side. I will force the Kuru Dynasty out of our kingdom."

Quinton walked to Death Claws. Death Claws said his name, then Smoke, Ryuu, Sandstorm said their names. Quinton got on Death Claws' back and was flying, while the rest of the dragons followed.

Quinton was flying around the city and saw the girl he had a crush on, Abijah, and had Death Claws pick her up. She held onto Quinton so tight, so he knew she was scared. People in the city were throwing roses at them, indicating them to get married. Quinton looked back at her, and she was smiling. They passed towns, villages, and cities, and people could not believe what was before their eyes. Kids were chasing after them, wanting to get on the dragons. People were amazed they were on the dragons. Quinton and Abijah smiled. They'd been in the air for some time.

"It's getting late. It's time to get you home and to get back to the city." Quinton took her home. He got a kiss, and he left happy.

Chapter 5

The next day, his grandfather died in his sleep. The people lit a candle for him. The the monks washed his body. Ezra was being viewed at the sacred house, and once everybody was done seeing him, he was carried to the water, and his body burned, drifting off in the sea. Ezra was one of God's messenger. He didn't want to be buried because people from the city would leave gifts on his grave or worship him at his grave site.

Once they were done with Ezra's body, his wish was for them to feast and be happy for him because he was in God hands. The people ate, sang, and dance, and talked about the good that came out of Ezra being God's messenger and how all the years Ezra prophesizing to them, they thought he was an insane man, but he was a gift from God.

Quinton got on his job and started God's work by sending messengers to deliver the messages to the Kuru King Ikshvaku, ruler over all the people, and to the cities, towns, and nearby villages. The Messengers came back with messages from the Kuru King and the people. The messages told the Dragon Emperor some people from the cities, towns, and villages submitted to monotheism, but the rest of the people rejected the monotheistic belief and were standing with the Kuru King.

"I will bring upon them God's punishment and drive paganism out of the country and make the whole country believers."

Quinton called upon the dragons. He mounted up on Death Claws while the rest of the dragons took off behind Death Claws. The first city they reached, the dragons flames ripped the city up in pieces and killed the pagans that were in the city. Quinton said to himself, "If only they would have submitted to monotheism, they would had been alive."

Every town and village Quinton reach, he destroyed. The Kuru Kingdom and army, he destroyed. The Kuru King and his remaining men retreated with him. The people started coming to the Holy City of Arunachal for refuge.

Once the Dragon Emperor gained control of the country, he had all the men who were strong build him a palace with well-equipped defense system out of the Holy City of Arunachal. Nobody dare faced the fire dragons or the Fire Dragon Army. The Emperor's palace had three walls, but nobody there to test his security or walls.

Time passed, and General Ghiath had the Fire Dragon Army trained to overcome any battle. The second war was to invade Jerusalem and push Rome out of Jerusalem. Rome been governing Jerusalem for a very long time. Quinton the Dragon Emperor left Snake Eyes the to protect the kingdom as well as his family, with 50,000 Fire Dragon soldiers and guards around the kingdom. Quinton the Dragon Emperor on Death Claws led Ryuu, Egan, Sandstorm, and 50,000 Fire Dragon soldiers to Jerusalem. Once they got to Roman camps, they torched all Roman camps.

Roman soldiers didn't know the wrath of God was coming, and the Roman soldiers died, screaming and running. Once the Roman soldiers retreated to Jerusalem, the Roman soldiers had heard what happened to their camps near to Jerusalem, and they fled and went to Greece with the Legions in Greece. Quinton the Dragon Emperor paid his respect and offered a ritual prayer to build the biggest holy sacred house of worship for monotheistic belief. Quinton the Dragon Emperor had a thousand of his men build the biggest worshiping place in the world. It took them months, but it was the most beautiful, holiest place in the world. It was named Euphrates, which means "break forth" or "river."

General Gaith informed the emperor, "Rome formed an army of 100,000 soldiers."

Quinton informed the General, "Gaith, get the men ready to sail to Greece."

When Quinton reached Greece, the Roman soldiers were ready for war. Even though the dragon military was outnumbered, they had dragons.

Death Claws led the attack. The flames came down on the Roman soldiers trying to use their shields, but the dragons' flames melted through their shields, disintegrating them and causing thousands of the Roman soldiers to die in seconds. The Roman army was too arrogant and prideful. They stood their ground, getting half their army slaughtered. Once the Roman General Hortensius died, they retreated. None of the Fire Dragon soldiers even picked up their swords or an arrow. They stood on guard, witnessing the slaughtering.

Once the Roman army retreated, Quinton the Dragon Emperor told the Greek people they were free under his conditions to pick a King and to build a sacred worship house for monotheistic belief. He told them, "Do not cause harm to my monks. I am going to leave them here to teach your people the religion with my soldiers protecting them."

The Greek people said, "That's all we have to do to be free? Pledge our oath to you?"

The Greek people pledged their loyalty to the Emperor to submit to monotheistic beliefs. The Fire Dragon soldiers and the Greek people started building the sacred house. Months of building and getting their votes together for the new king of Greece took place.

Roman Republicans heard what happened to one of their strongest armies, so the Roman Emperor left it in the Republican hands. The Roman Republicans put out a bounty on Quinton the Dragon Emperor's head for enough gold to buy a country and build an army. The angels informed the Emperor the plot. The rebel army came to Greece's doorstep, and the General Gaith informed the Dragon Emperor to let him destroy the bandits. Quinton the Dragon Emperor allowed General Gaith to deal with the issue. General Gaith left on Ryuu with Sandstorm on the side and 30,000 Fire Dragon soldiers. Ryuu and Sandstorm's flames came down on Rome's hired army, and the flames disintegrated the men. Sorcerers saw the dragons and could not believe it; they retreated, and the General sent 20,000 soldiers shooting arrows while the other 10,000 on horses waited to plunge into the dying men on fire. The arrows kept coming, and Ryuu and Sandstorm kept flames coming down on them like lava coming out of a volcano. Once the rest of the men started to flee, General Gaith pulled back. Quinton the Dragon Emperor heard about the defeat and made the General the number-two man in his kingdom.

Time passed, the sacred House was built, and the emperor left 10,000 Fire Dragon soldiers there and appointed another General by the name of Alexander, then went back to his kingdom.

Quinton was growing strong and looked like his father with long hair and full facial hair, and he was a great fighter like his father. Abijah was a woman every woman wanted to be like and look like. Quinton and her married, so she was the empress of the Fire Dragon people. From all over the country, Jerusalem, and Greece, people brought gifts to them and food for the dragons. Abijah was grateful. Quinton was fulfilling some of his grandfather prophecies from God. Quinton trained Abijah to be a great swordswoman.

She and the Emperor had twins that were now eight years old. Uzza was the boy, and he was a Dragon King. Yara, she is the girl, and she's a Dragon Queen. The dragons had two babies, Egan and Malinda; both were closed to Uzza and Yara. The third kid was Khadijah; she was five years old. She played alone because her brother and sister did not like playing with her.

Abijah was about to give birth to another child. General Gaith informed the Emperor, "King Gilgamesh is oppressing his people and is a pagan King."

Quinton ordered one of his messengers to take a note to the city of Uruk and inform King Gilgamesh. The messenger was scared of the giant king. The messenger left right away, and when he got to Uruk, he was escorted to King Gligamesh. The messenger gave the note to King Gligamesh. The note read:

> *I am the Dragon Emperor, and I was given a dream by God Almighty and was told to inform you to stop oppressing your people and worshipping other gods and submit to the one true God.*

King Gilgamesh ripped the note up, then ordered his men to chop off the messenger's head and send it back to the Dragon Emperor. Quinton got the messenger's head as a warning from King Gilgamesh to install fear in the Emperor, but King Gilgamesh didn't realize Quinton was the Emperor over dragons and had the very powerful Dragon Sword.

The Dragon Emperor mounted up on Death Claw, and once the dragons reach Uruk, the King Gligamesh couldn't believe what was before his eyes. His men fired arrows, but the arrows didn't penetrate the dragons' hides. The battle didn't last long. The dragons' flames ripped through the Uruk Kingdom, but the King escaped through the tunnels under the palace. He didn't get far; the palace and the tunnels were destroyed, and the king was killed by the palace and the tunnels collapsing on him from the dragon flames. The people of Uruk were running scared and crying while the Fire Dragon Army killed all the soldiers of King Gligamesh and destroyed the city. King Gligamesh's people were taken to India to live. The Dragon Emperor got people's attention all over the world by destroying Uruk in just under a little bit of time.

When Quinton got back to his kingdom, his wife Abijah gave birth to a boy. She gave him the name Ibrahim. Abijah could not have any more kids, for her womb was unable to bear another child. Uzza was upset because he wasn't the only boy. When Quinton got back from Uruk, he was welcomed with another son, and he was so please with him. While holding him in his arms, he prayed to God to protect his son and to bless him with an offspring who could bear the sword after him. Quinton spent years pushing the Romans out of countries with their pagan beliefs.

Quinton's son Uzza was forced to marry a young girl named Keturah for getting her pregnant. Quinton was upset because his first grandson was made without the parents being married, so he wanted his grandson to be born with both of the parents being married, so God would not be upset with his family. Both of them got married in the palace; they feasted after the wedding. By Quinton taking control of India and have dragons, he had the strongest army in the world.

One of the Dragon Emperor's men picked up his sword, and the sword froze the man to death. The men knew only the Chosen One could bear the sword. The whole country heard about what happened and got their mind off trying to steal the sword to have control of the dragons. They feared the sword and the dragons.

Time passed, and a horseman came riding to the palace of the Dragon Emperor with an urgent message. The soldiers ask the man who summoned him there. The man told them he was Prophet Shan.

When the soldiers heard the prophet's name, they let the prophet through the gate.

The emperor saw the prophet and gave him a hug. The prophet told him the city of Reykjavik in Iceland's people were being kill by ice dragons. Quinton informed his family that he was going to Iceland to stop the ice dragons from eating the people and control them. He left his son, King Uzza, in charge of the kingdom. His wife knew this was some of the prophecy. He kissed his wife and the kids and took Death Claw, Smoke, and 100 Dragon Soldiers dressed in black leather with a red dragon on their uniforms.

Chapter 6

They reached Thule, which was in Iceland, and landed in the city of Reykjavik. The people were running, pointing at the Dragon Emperor. The people were amazed, looking at the dragons with armor and the Dragon Emperor on a saddle on the dragon, and the Fire Dragon soldiers were moving in a formation they'd never seen before. The Dragon Emperor landed in front the sacred house, and the monk came out and welcomed him and his men. They set up camp around the city. The people were saying, "It's true, the Dragon Emperor came to save us from the ice dragons! He has the sword that can kill the dragons."

Death Claw and Smoke were flying around, and the people notices Death Claw and Smoke had saddles on their back and looked different from the ice dragons. Quinton came out of the sacred house, and the people were outside in crowds. He told the people he was the Dragon Emperor, and God granted him the power to talk to the dragons and a sword to control them or kill them if they resisted. He spotted a woman who took his breath away. She was a daughter of the Master Carpenter of the city. She smiled at him. He walked up to her, and she said, "I've been hearing stories about you conquering countries and how you've got dragons under your control. Now, I see it for my own eyes."

"What's your name?"

"Delilah."

"I am going to make you my second wife."

"How is that?"

"Because your city is going to owe me something once I save the people here, and you are what I want, and to build a kingdom here of God fearing people."

"Maybe you'll get your prize. Let's see…*after* you save the city."

"I am going to have you control the ice dragons with me, and the new kingdom I am going to build here."

"We will see."

He mounted up on Death Claw and went to the Reykjavik mountains where the dragons lived. When he got close to the cave where they lived, the ice dragons came out of the cave to fight. Once they saw Death Claw and Smoke, they breathed ice at the fire dragons. The fire dragons melted the ice. They kept on doing that until Quinton started talking to them. The ice dragons didn't want to submit and be under his control, but once he pulled the Dragon Sword out, they backed up. The ice dragons' leader, Naga, tried to attack Quinton and freeze him, but Quinton shot fire out the sword to stop the freeze,

Once Quinton sent water at Naga, knocking Naga over, Naga couldn't move, and so Naga gave up and submitted, and the rest of the dragons followed along. They all bowed down. The Dragon Emperor was flying with the ice dragons to show the people of Reykjavik City he had the ice dragons under control. He landed where his men were holding camp. The city people brought the dragons food, and he had his soldiers go to the four corners of Iceland and inform the pagan people and the barbarians to submit to the one true God of the heavens of the Earth and everything between. The Dragons Emperor would have mercy on their tribes if they did so. They laughed and told the Fire Dragon soldiers to leave before they die.

The Emperor's soldiers informed him what the people said, and he ordered the dragons to burn and freeze the pagans until they submitted. Some of the barbarians escaped to Greenland. The Dragon Emperor slaughtered different tribes, killing their leaders and King Arvid, who was over the tribes. Iceland was under the control of the Dragon Emperor. The Emperor sent for 100,000 soldiers to come from India, Greece, and Jerusalem to move into Greenland and Norway to crush the barbarians before they attack Iceland's people. The Dragon Emperor had men working day and night to build him a palace that could withstand any attack.

CHAPTER 7

It took them months to build the palace and to prepare for war against Greenland barbarians and Norway barbarians. The barbarians' army equaled 200,000 soldiers, while the Dragon Emperor's army equaled close to 110,000 soldiers with six ice dragons and two fire dragons. The Dragon Emperor sent spies to spy on the brothers of King Arvid. King Asger's men came in from Norway to join his brother, King Asmund, in Greenland. The Empress Delilah of Iceland was pregnant. The Empress Abijah accepted her husband's wishes and knew he was allowed to have many wives as he wanted.

The Dragon King Uzza brought his son Ishmael to be blessed by his grandfather, the Emperor of the Dragons. The Emperor blessed the baby. When the King Uzza saw his father had a new wife and she was pregnant, he got upset that his father have another kid on the way, and it could be a chance that kid would bear the sword and not him. King Uzza wanted to be the one bear the sword once his father departed to be with God. The Emperor saw it in his face when he introduced King Uzza to his other wife, Delilah, and the unborn boy in her stomach.

The Emperor told his family, "Let's feast as one family. I saw this in a dream God's given me. To be sitting here with my family that's growing." The Emperor told his son, King Uzza, to sit next to him to give him some words of wisdom. The Emperor leaned over and whispered into his ears, "God sees all things and chooses who he want to bear the sword. Everything I am doing is a commandment from the God of men and jinns. When I do things that are not according to God's will, he will leave my side and take everything away from me. Be patient, and trust in God." He then smiled at his father, then start eating.

Days passed, and he informed his son to go back home with his wife and son and run the Kingdom of Arunachal, and when he need him, he would send for him. King Uzza went back home upset; he wanted to be a part of the war. The Dragon Emperor met with the barbarians' army in the area called Nuuk. Both armies faced each other; the Dragon Emperor had dragons; the barbarians' army had dragon-killing harpoon stations on wheels.

The Emperor went in the air with the dragons and froze and burned most of the harpoon stations while the dragons ducked and swerved around the deadly harpoons. The fire dragons burned the barbarians, turning them into ashes. Then the Emperor sent in his foot calvary; there were heads, arms, and body parts flying everywhere, and then the horseman charged into the battle. Men were falling down on both sides, dying. The Dragon Emperor blew the horn, and his men pulled back, then the archers sent arrows, killing barbarians. The barbarians rushed towards the Dragon Emperor's army. The ice dragons froze them, and the fire dragons disintegrated them. The barbarians retreated, but the emperor pursued and killed King Asger. King Asmund retreated back to Norway. King Asmund sent his sister as an offering of marriage, and his kingdom would submit to monotheistic belief.

The Emperor kept Queen Aslaug safe. Once his son, King Ibraham, arrived, the emperor presented Queen Aslaug to King Ibrahim as his wife, and he liked her. Aslaug was a redhead, very beautiful and a great warrior that the barbarians' respect. The both of them would rule over Norway and Greenland with monotheistic beliefs. Aslaug was happy with King Ibrahim as her husband, and both of them ruled Greenland and Norway now. Once the Emperor put Greenland in order, he went to Norway with both rulers to take their rightful place in Norway. He met with King Asmund to discuss the terms of King Ibrahim and Queen Aslaug's ruling. King Asmund had no problem with his sister taking over for him to live. King Asmund went into retirement and stood by his sister's side. The barbarians and Dragon Army built the King and Queen a palace and a sacred house for the monks to teach monotheism. The King and Queen got two palaces, one in Greenland and Norway.

The Emperor invaded most of the countries in what we call today North America, South America, and Central America, and defeated all of the barbarian armies, causing them to submit to monotheism. Time passed, and Empress Delilah's son, King Maximus, was three years old now, and her daughter, Queen Elizabeth, was one year old. King Ibrahim's son, Gaius, by Queen Aslaug was two years old now, and King Ibrahim's daughter Josephine was one year old. King Uzza's daughter Amina was four years old. The Emperor was informed the Qin Dynasty sent request for the Emperor to bow down to the Emperor of China and demanded the people of India to pay taxes to the Qin Dynasty. The Qin Dynasty wanted to rule the world, and they were killing other rulers and putting them under their pagan belief. The Emperor denied the Qin Emperor's offer and told him they would meet and battle, and that's where they would see who was the ruler of the world and who would be paying taxes.

Chapter 8

The Qin Dynasty met the Emperor on the battlefield with 300,000 soldiers and Godzillas and King Kongs. The Dragon Emperor had 200,000 Fire Dragon soldiers and dragons. The Fire Dragon General Gaith had the soldiers moving in box formation with shields and armor protecting the body in the head, and archers behind them. Once they met the Qin Dynasty in the middle of the battlefield, the Qin military could not penetrate the box formation.

The General sent his horsemen; the Fire Dragon military still was winning when the Qin military started firing fireballs of flaming oil and using dynamite. The ice dragons froze the fire balls. The Emperor got tired of fighting fear. The fire dragons started disintegrating the Qin military, and the Emperor Qin Shi Hang was the only one that have control over the beasts Godzilla and King Kong; he sent them to attack the dragons. The ice dragons froze King Kong; Godzillas sent fire at the ice dragons. Death Claw's flames came down on Godzilla, then Godzilla was in flames, hollering in flames, and he fell over. Smoke's flames finished the Godzilla. The other King Kong was pushing and crushing the dragon soldiers, then the ice dragons all froze King Kong. The Dragon Emperor's sword grew long and cut both of Godzilla's legs off, then the sword set him on fire. The Qin Emperor saw the power the sword had, so he had his men wave the white flag. The Dragon Emperor and the Qin Emperor sat down with one another in a tent. The Qin Emperor offered both of his daughters, Princess Husting and Princess Huayang, and he also told the Dragon Emperor he saw the sword in his dream and didn't believe the sword existed, and whoever bore the sword, he willing follow the belief of. The Qin Emperor interpreted his dream to the Dragon Emperor. The Dragon Emperor accepted Princess Husting and Princess Huayang. The Dragon Emperor married both of the Qin Emperor's daughters and laid with both of them. The Dragon Emperor stood with the Emperor of the Qin Dynasty for some time. Both of his daughters had kids by the Dragon Emperor. Empress Huating had a boy, Yuzhang, who was now three years old, and daughter, Wu Zetian, who was one year old; and Empress Huayang had a girl, Fu Hao, who was three years old, and a boy, Su Wu, who was one year old. Emperor Qin Shi Hang was happy his descendants were growing and had the bloodline to control the dragons and the Dragon Sword. The ice dragons were sent back to Iceland with both of the empress wives Delilah and Abijah.

Water Dragons causing floods in the southern part of Africa killing Zimbabwe people. The Dragon Emperor was informed by Prophet Shan to help the Kingdom of Zimbabwe from the water dragons, as the people had been of monotheistic belief for some time. Zimbabwe people saw the Dragon Emperor on Death Claw and Smoke on the other side, and they were scared and couldn't believe they were different dragons from the water dragons coming from Victoria Falls, and a man was on the back of a dragon. When the Dragon Emperor landed in the town of Chimanimani, a monk approached him because the people were scared, but the monk knew God was going to send help one day, and he believed the day was today when he saw a man on a saddle on the back of a dragon. The Dragon Emperor informed the monk in a language he was familiar with that he was a messenger of God, and he was sent to help the Zimbabwe Kingdom become a kingdom of God. God had heard the people's cries. The monk explained to the people what the Dragon Emperor said, and the people welcomed him to their people. The Dragon Emperor was taken to the sacred house. The Emperor pulled out the Dragon Sword and informed them the sword had power to control dragons of all species, and he added, "I am the only one who can bear the sword. If anyone picks up my sword, they will die."

The monks said, "We will inform the people to not touch the sword, and you are God's messenger sent with the sword that controls the dragons and can kill the dragons." Once the monk informed the people the Dragon Emperor was there to help them, they start cheering. Death Claw was looking at them, making sure nothing happened to the Dragon Emperor. He told Death Claw, "Everything is alright."

Dragon Emperor went to Victoria Falls where the water dragons were at. When the Dragon Emperor got to Victoria Falls, the water dragons smelled Death Claw and Smoke, so they came out to attack the fire dragons. Smoke's flames burned one of the water dragons, killing the dragon. The water dragons knocked smoke out of the air with water coming from all sides and with enough force to knock down trees. Death Claw went to send fire flames, but the Dragon Emperor stopped him and took out his sword and told them in dragon tongue, he was bearing the Dragon Sword. The water dragons knew the Dragon Sword possessed many great powers. The dragons bowed down, but one of the water dragons didn't believe Quinton the Dragon Emperor was bearing the sword; he refuse, so the Dragon Emperor cut him out of the air, then froze the remains and shot fire to the sky, showing the water dragons that the sword in his hand was the Dragon Sword. All the water dragons bow down. Once he got control of the water dragons, the people of Zimbabwe fed them sheep and cows. The Emperor Mujahid from Ethiopia found out about the Dragon Emperor saving Zimbabwe from the water dragons that had been causing chaos for centuries, and he ordered to see him.

The Dragon Emperor was led by the monks to visit Emperor Mujahid. When the Dragon Emperor got to Ethiopia, the people were in shock to see how the Emperor had control over all the water dragons he bought with him. They were throwing rose petals and enchanting the savior of Africa. The Emperor Mujahid hugged the Dragon Emperor and told him, "My people love you for what you've done for our country. I am grateful God brought you to our lands to save the African people, and I am grateful I am a believer and not a pagan because I would not want to feel God's wrath through your hands and the dragons. I know you sit here as my brother. This my daughter, Queen Esther, and my son, King Umar, I heard you have many children. I want to marry my children to yours, and they can rule Africa together and control the dragons together in Africa."

"I will love that," Emperor Quinton replied, "but under one condition."

"What is that?" Emperor Mujahid said.

"We must wage war on the idol worshippers. God's work is first."

"I agree."

"My men and the dragons are ready for war. You give me the coordinates to the place where pagans are, and I will invade those places and get them to submit to God under our belief system, then leave a monk and soldiers in every city, town, and village to get the religion to the people."

Emperor Mujahid replied, "My general, Malik, will assist you with half my army and 25 of my monks."

"I will have your people communicate with my people," General Malik said.

The Dragon Emperor sent his General Gaith with General Malik and half of the Dragon Army and four water dragons to get the rest of Africa to accept monotheistic beliefs while Emperor Quinton stood with Emperor Mujahid awaiting his family to arrive. Emperor Mujahid sent letters to all the kings of Africa and told them to give up their fake gods and submit to the one God of the heavens and the Earth.

"As you are reading this letter, my army and the Dragon Army are coming to all your doorsteps to make sure your people give up their false gods and accept the one true God of Abraham by submitting to monotheistic belief. Our monks will teach you the monotheistic belief."

All the kings and rulers were scared of the dragons and the mighty army that was close to their doorstep.

Chapter 9

The Dragon Emperor's wives and children arrived with the fire dragons and ice dragons. Emperor Mujahid was amazed to see King Uzza's soldiers' armor was red, and the fire dragon saddles were red. The soldiers from Iceland's armor was blue, and the ice dragon saddles were blue. Emperor Mujahid turned to the Dragon Emperor and said, "Our colors should be white like the water dragons. White is a pure color, and we are pure children of God."

"Yes, we are. We will have that arranged," the Dragon Emperor said. He introduced his wives and children to Emperor Mujahid, and the Emperor gave them his blessings and introduced his family. King Umar smiled at Yara, and the family saw that King Umar liked Yara, and Yara liked him. Days passed, and Queen Yara married King Umar, and King Uzza married Queen Esther; she became his second wife. The generals came back with great news. All the countries, cities, towns, and villages accepted monotheism. The men built sacred houses for the monks to teach the people. Time passed. The Emperors sacrificed two lambs, giving thanks to God for the blessings. Yara gave birth to a boy named Sadiq.

Queen Blue Sky had a girl, Helen. Queen Shiba gave birth to a boy, Titan. Emperor Mujahid was filled with so much joy. Emperor Quinton ordered his son, King Uzza, to take his family back to India and rule over the people.

"When I need you, I will call for you."

It was bedtime emperor, and Quinton was blessed from God to please all his empresses. They waited one at a time, getting pleasure from their emperor husband, then they slept sound asleep to the morning. The generals came back with great news; the people accepted the religion and didn't put up a fight.

"Through God's will, the people submitted," the Dragon Emperor said. It was time to leave back to Iceland. The Dragon Emperor left a legion of 5,000 Water Dragon soldiers in white leather armor and two water dragons, Hydro and Rainstorm, and one fire dragon, Malinda.

The Emperor and his family boarded their ships, traveling back to Iceland through the bad weather, and made it back to Iceland. The people were so happy to see the Emperor and the royal family, they were bringing food for the dragons. Nyres, Neutral, Hatuibwari, and Hyperion, they were taking to their new home in the Skogafoo Waterfalls. The Dragon Emperor had his General Gaith gather soldiers from all the countries they ruled. The General gathered 300,000 soldiers. The Emperor wanted them to attack Rome.

The Roman Emperor, Diocletian, heard about the Dragon Emperor coming to attack Rome if the Roman people did not submit to God of Abraham, who created heavens and Earth and all creations. Emperor Diocletian believed he was above God and worshipped many pagan gods, and some of the Roman people followed the god of Abraham in secret. Roman military was on standby. When Rome's military saw all the dragons they'd been hearing about, they wondered how they could win the war against the Dragon Emperor. The Emperor of Rome knew if he went against the Fire Dragon Army, he was not going to have a kingdom, so he turned to the senators. The senators were conniving and wanted nothing but wealth no matter the cost; they know they could not win the war, and the Roman people would be slaughtered. The Roman people heard about the Emperor's military and dragons heading towards Rome. They were panicking. The Senators informed the people, "The Dragon Emperor is a reasonable man. We ordered for him to sit down with us and reason with us. Ever country he conquered, he just wanted the people to submit to the God over all gods, and for the people to build a sacred house for his monks to teach the people how to worship the God over all the gods."

The people shouted out, "Give him what he wants, so we can live!"

The emperor shouted out, "We will build his secret house and let the people worship his God."

The Dragon Emperor arrived in Rome, and the senators requested to sit down with him.

On the Roman senators' floor, the Dragon Emperor sat down with the Roman Emperor and the senators.

"I am Quinton, the Dragon Emperor. I was chosen by God and given the Dragon Sword to control the dragons and bring the wrath upon all pagans on Earth." When the Emperor and the senators saw the Dragon Sword changing different elements, they knew it came from some high power. "I want a sacred house for God's monks, and all citizens to submit to monotheistic belief in God. The monks will teach them monotheism. Do we have an agreement? If I leave here without the Emperor Diocletian and the senators complying with my offers, I will have my dragons destroy Rome forever."

The senators looked at Emperor Diocletian. He waved his hand, indicating "go ahead," and the senators put all the Dragon Emperor's demands in writing, and it became law. The Roman people were happy they weren't going to be destroyed by the dragons. The people of Rome built the Dragon Emperor a house outside of Rome. The Dragon Emperor brought his family to attend his celebration of conquering Rome. Once they were done celebrating, he spent time with his wives and kids. After months of being with his family, he ordered his family to leave back to Iceland. The Dragon Emperor inform General Gaith to get the military ready for Egypt: "We go to war with the Pharaoh. He refuses to give up his gods."

CHAPTER 10

The Dragon Emperor on Death Claw was with the rest of the dragons, who were ready to kill everything in sight and eat the remains of people. Pharaoh's army was ready. The sorcerers sent out big scorpions and spiders, but the dragons burned them and ate them. Pharaoh's army pushed forward, and the Dragon Army pushed forward. They clashed into each other like rams. Bodies were everywhere. The General Ghiath had the army pull back, and the dragons sent flames, killing hundreds of men instantly, then the dragons started eating the dead bodies. Pharaoh saw the dragons eating his men, so he walked out to the Dragon Emperor and bowed down. His men followed suit and bowed down.

The Dragon Emperor accepted the defeat and sat down with Pharaoh Ptolemy I Philadelphus. The Dragon Emperor told the Pharaoh he wanted all his sorcerers to be put to death and all the false idols destroyed, and he wanted a sacred house to be built for the people to worship the true God of all living things. The Emperor informed the Pharaoh he was going to summon one of his daughters, Queen Khadijah, to offer her as one of his wives, to help him govern the religion and the new way of life for the Egypt people. The Pharaoh accept the Dragon Emperor offer. The Dragon Emperor summoned his family, and they arrived with the rest of the dragons and 1,000 soldiers. Queen Khadijah accepted the marriage. The Dragon Emperor and his family stayed in Egypt until Queen Khadijah married and had a child. She name him Ali, and the Dragon Emperor left behind two legions of 10,000 soldiers and four water dragons: Viper, Rhaegal, Haku, Hellos, and a fire dragon, Snake Eyes.

The Dragon Emperor went back to the Iceland kingdom. While sitting on his throne, the country people brought court issues. The first case a man brought to the Emperor about bandit stealing his crops and animals. The Emperor ordered 10 of his soldiers to investigate the issue. The second case was from a woman by the name of Adina. She stood in front of the Emperor for murdering her abusive husband.

"Who are the witnesses?"

"The deceased's sister Hosanna and the servant Naarah. I stand here to let the court know, my brother was very abusive and allowed the alcohol take control of him. Adina was home waiting on my brother when he came home drunk and start beating on Adina. She hit him on the side of the head with a statue, and he fell back and hit his head on the table and stopped breathing."

The next witness was the servant.

"What's your name?"

"Naarah."

"What did you witness?"

"I saw my master come in the house drunk and start beating on Adina. He grabbed the statue, and both of them fell to the floor. Adina got the statue before my master could get it, she got up. My master rushed towards her, and she swung the statue, hitting him on the head. He fell and hit his head on the table and stopped breathing."

"Okay, thank you. My judgment in this case is that Adina did not have the attention to kill her husband. It's self-defense, release her, and let her go home to her kids."

Adina was crying, holding her kids. The people from the city called the Emperor a just ruler. The Emperor's men were successful in the investigation of finding out who was the one behind the stealing the crops in the animals, and the Emperor's men cut his hands off and let him go.

The people started building their houses out of bricks to give the house better support. The Emperor had his soldiers go around the country, taking people food who didn't have food, and the people wanted to join the military to have better lives for their families.

Emperor Quinton got a message from the prophet Shan to invade Persia. Quinton ordered the General Gaith to get the men ready for war with the Persian King Seleucus. General Gaith gathered 200,000 soldiers in black leather armor with a red dragon on their armor. The Dragon Army crossed over the Persian Gulf into Persian territory to meet the awaiting the Persian army's 300,000 soldiers. The King knew he had the numbers in men, but what he didn't know was the dragons killed the whole armies themselves. The Emperor held back his dragons and watched his men fight for hours until the Persian army was defeated.

King Ibrahim was forcing the pagans out of New Zealand. The barbarians' war tactics got them to keep the war going for three days, but King Ibrahim was fighting without the dragons to show his father he was a true warrior, and he could be a conqueror by forcing the heathen pagans out of their lands and to worship the one true God who created the heavens and Earth. Once the war was won, they had their army build a palace that could withstand attack from the Pagans and their enemies. King Ibrahim's wife, Queen Aslaug, picked another wife for him because she cannot bear anymore children. King Ibrahim was happy with his wife's pick, a woman from the barbarians named Blue Sky. Her eyes were blue, and her beauty captivated him, and her body had him hypnotized. After he married her, he laid with her.

When his father Quinton heard his son conquered New Zealand and wed another wife, he was proud of him and sent him two strong Persian horses and two Persian woman servants. When King Uzza heard about his brother King Ibrahim conquering New Zealand, he had envy and malice in his heart, knowing his brother was getting more blessings from his father. King Uzza was king over the Kingdom of Arunachal, while King Ibrahim ruled Norway, Greenland, and New Zealand. The people loved him as their ruler.

CHAPTER 11

In Persia, Emperor Quinton had his men build him a palace bigger them all his palaces, and the wall around the palace was built so no army could penetrate it, and the soil around the palace was rich and cultivated. The servants grew rich crops for the Emperor. The animals lived in barns and had their own area. They built their own running water system underground that went to the palace and the barn, and all the soldiers built a houses outside the palace. The dragons lived beneath the palace in caves that led to the outside. Once the cave doors opened, the dragons roamed around freely. The water dragons were stressed in the cold, so they were brought to Persia and housed under the palace away from the fire dragons. The water dragons' food source came from the Mediterranean Sea.

Quinton the Dragon Emperor had his four wives pick two Persian women to marry and have kids. His wives picked two Persian women named Nadia and Soraya, both brown skinned in complexion with silky, long hair to their lower back. They looked like Egyptian women. The Emperor laid with them to have Persian offspring to rule Persia.

Time passed, and Nadia had two kids by the Emperor. Jasmine, who was now nine years old, and Saam, who was seven years old. Soraya had two children also, named Suri, nine years old, and Abbas eight years old. The Emperor's children had more kids. King Ibrahim of Norway and other countries' wife Queen Blue Sky had a son, nine years old, named Azam. Queen Khadijah from Egypt had a daughter named Alma who's eight years old. Queen Yara of Ethiopia had a daughter named

Amira who's nine years old as well. The dragons had more dragons: The water dragons had Waves and Vector, the fire dragons, Hellfire and Lava, and the ice dragons, Stormbreaker and Frozen.

Maximus was the king of Iceland, and his sister Queen Elizabeth helped him rule Iceland. Between Maximus and his brother, King Ibrahim, they had the ice dragons under their control, while King Uzza of India had three fire dragons (Egan, Dragor, and Lava) and two water dragons (Nyres and Neutral). In Africa, Yara had one fire dragon, Malinda, and two water dragons, Hydro and Rainstorm. China did not have dragons because the Emperor kids weren't their rulers.

People from all over the world were coming to trade in Persia and to see the dragons and the Dragon Emperor's new kingdom. The people were moving with no worries around the kingdom and knew the Dragon Emperor was God's messenger and had heard the angels were protesting him

His kingdom was the safest kingdom in the world. In the Dragon Emperor Colosseum, before the games started, the Dragon Emperor showed up on Death Claw and showed the people the power of the sword. The sword extended fire across the Colosseum; he froze a pail of water hooked to the back of a chariot. The people were amazed when the Emperor shot water out of the sword, and it came down on all the people in the Colosseum, like it was a sudden rain cloud passing, and left drops of rain on the people. The people were shocked once they knew it was water. They all started laughing. Then the games begin. Arrow bullseye out from far, wrestling matches; medieval sports of jousting, spear competitions, sword fighting, and men fighting to the death that were sentenced under their laws to death. Whoever won was free; the who one died have received his sentence.

Chapter 12

King Ibrahim and Queen Aslaug invaded Gaul with their Ice Dragon Army. The Arverni tribe stayed out of open ground because the dragons could attack them, so they used guerrilla warfare and fought in the woods. The Arverni tribe came face-to-face with King Ibrahim in the woods, and barbarians stood there with their faces colored, yelling; archers in the trees and men in tunnels. The siege began. The Dragon Army men stood in box formation with shields protecting them with archers in the middle of them, but the barbarians were attacking the Ice Dragon soldiers from under them until the Ice Dragon soldiers just got into the tunnels. King Ibrahim sent in his knights and archers behind the knights, and they left bodies everywhere. The people gave up once King Ibrahim pushed them out of the woods into an open area and saw the dragons. King Ibrahim got control of the country. He stood there and made everyone submit to monotheism, then appointed monks and had the people build a sacred house and palace. Queen Aslaug was ruling Norway and Greenland. Queen Blue Sky ruled New Zealand.

Time passed. King Ibrahim wed a woman named Rika from the Arverni tribe who was very beautiful. Quinton the Dragon Emperor arrived with his wives and kids to support King Ibrahim and give him his blessing. King Ibrahim had a feast for his family. King Ibrahim sat down with his father and showed him on the map two countries with barbarian pagans. He wanted to invade Myrrh, which is Ireland today, and Scotland. His father informed him to let his brother, King Maximus and his sister Queen Elizabeth carry out the siege. King Ibrahim replied, "If that's what you want. King Maximus and Queen Elizabeth can carry out the siege."

"Before you tell them, I want you to know, I am proud of you. You are now a ruler of four great Kingdoms."

King Ibrahim hugged his father and told him that meant a lot to him, hearing those words come out of his mouth from him. King Ibrahim went to get his brother and sister and took them to his war chambers. He showed them the first war they were going to carry out, and he going to be by their side.

"Father told me to give each one of ya'll the countries."

Both of them were excited about their first invasion.

King Uzza sent his family to give his brother blessings and never showed up because he was preparing for a siege, and he didn't want to be around his brother King Ibrahim's celebration because it was supposed to be him conquering countries, not his little brother.

The General Gaith gave the Dragon Emperor a note from General Alexander:

> *I am writing you to inform you, King Amyntas was poisoned by his own people, and he does not have a successor because he had all girls.*

Quinton wrote back to General Alexander:

> *You kept the country safe. You are king and I want you to marry the previous king's daughters.*

Signed and sealed by the Emperor.

The high Monk read the note to the people:

"For killing y'all's king, the General Alexander will be the successor for King Amyntas, and the princesses will be his Queens."

The people cheered for Alexander. Time passed. The new King Alexander was crowned, and his three wives were also crowned. It was the first time in history to see three queens ruling at the same time.

CHAPTER 13

Quinton the Dragon Emperor made it back to Persia with his family. The Persians were throwing rose petals at the royal family. As they were making their way through the gates, the Emperor made his way into the palace to eat and bathe. King Ibrahim, King Maximus, and Queen Elizabeth were facing a combined force of the Celtic tribes. They sent in the archers, then the knights followed the foot soldiers, killing Celtic barbarians. The Ice Dragon soldiers in their blue leather kept pushing barbarians back, and the barbarians were no match for the Ice Dragon soldiers. The Celtic tribes surrendered and accepted the monotheistic beliefs. The Celtics were scared of the ice dragons. They stood in shock when they saw the ice dragons King Maximus gained control of Ireland, he had his men build a palace strong enough to withstand any siege with two walls around the palace, and he had his men build a sacred house and had the monks guide the Celtic people to the belief. King Maximus stood in Ireland with 20,000 men and Stormbreaker, Frozen, and Desert Storm. Freeze, Eingana, and Hail left with Queen Elizabeth and 100,000 Ice Dragon soldiers in blue leather heading towards Scotland.

King Loarn Mac Eire of Dal Riata heard about the great Ice Dragon soldiers and heading his way. King Loarn Mac Eire knew the dragon armies were ruling the world, and all they wanted was for the King and his people to accept their religion and worship their God. At the thought of him losing his country and his life, he'd rather give them what they wanted, and when they came, he gave them what they wanted. The Ice Dragon army made their way to Dal Riata and saw there was no resistance. King Ibrahim told his Sister Queen Elizabeth, "You maybe got a kingdom without a fight. Let's see how you deal with these barbarians."

Queen Elizabeth rode out to King Loarn Mac Eire. King Loarn Mac Eire was the most handsome man she'd ever laid eyes on. They sat down and came to agreement: he and his people were going to accept her religion and allowed her monks to teach people the religion and build sacred houses for the people to pray in, only if she allowed him to be by her side as a friend.

Queen Elizabeth in blue leather armor with her bodyguards and a whole army were on his door steps.

"I want to get straight to the point: your people are pagans. They are worshiping what God created instead of God Almighty who created everything in our existence. I am only going to negotiate only once with you. If you and your people betray me, I will slaughter all your people."

"I am here with no resistance and at your mercy and am willing to swear an oath to you, but you must help me get the rest of the Scottish people in line," King Loarn Mac Eire said.

Queen Elizabeth said, "Okay, King Loarn Mac Eire. Kneel down on one knee and swear to accept monotheism, and we will fight against the people who will not join you in monotheistic belief."

The monks baptized King Loarn Mac Eire and his people, and their clothes were changed to the blue leather armor. The people were standing around the dragons in amazement to see the power Queen Elizabeth had. King Ibrahim kissed his sister goodbye and left with half the army. Queen Elizabeth had her men build her a palace while King Loarn Mac Eire hung around her and was very charming to her. She allowed him to get on one of her dragons to get the people to join them; some people joined while the rest went in hiding.

Time passed. The men got the palace and the sacred houses built up. In a year, the people of Scotland knew Queen Elizabeth was remaining in Scotland. Men were in hiding, trying to get in Ireland, but Ireland was surrounded with Ice Dragon soldiers. Some of the men came out of hiding and submitted to Queen Elizabeth. King Maximus married a Celtic warrior woman named Sahara, and the Celtic people in Ireland join him in his belief. King Loarn Mac Eire got Queen

Elizabeth's attention by charming her and gaining her trust by proving his loyalty. They got married.

The Celtic tribe was rebellious. The Ice Dragon soldiers covered all of Scotland and found the remaining barbarians. The ice dragons froze them and ate the rest of the rebels. Queen Elizabeth gained control of the hold Scotland. The Fire Dragons Emperor came to Scotland to see what Queen Elizabeth had done in Scotland and to give her his blessing and gifts. Queen Elizabeth was so happy to see her father.

The Scottish people heard about the Emperor, and for the first time, they were seeing him. The Fire Dragon army was in red leather armor. The Emperor gave Queen Elizabeth two Persian horses, a woman and male servant, and Persian jewels. She loved the gifts. She walked with her father and told him, "I want you to always be proud of me. If you see me doing something wrong, tell me. I would listen."

"I'm proud of you. I just want you to be safe and know I have an angel watching all your steps. I will tell you if something's wrong."

"That's great."

"God chose us," the Dragon Emperor said.

As Queen Elizabeth was coming back with our father, she told her servants to sacrifice two lambs to give a thanks to God. They ate and celebrated.

On the Roman senators' floors: "We are the Roman people. We conquered many countries, and Emperor Quinton took them. We're losing a lot of money. We need to come up with a method of hiring some sorcerers out there to help us kill these dragons."

"Senator Optimus, if you can come up with something to kill the dragons, we can work on building a massive army, and we still have people from the countries Emperor Quinton conquered who will rebel and turn on him."

"You know he has fire dragons, ice dragons, and water dragons, and his God on his side, and a very powerful Dragon Sword that he the only one can bear it. If the Senate's plan does not work, we all die," said the Emperor of Rome. "Senator Titus, Senator Optimus, have the majority votes to come up with a plan to find someone to kill the dragons and build the massive army."

Chapter 14

King Uzza invaded Indonesia, where the Kuru King retreated from India. He had soldiers attack Jakarta, Yogyakarta Bali, and Gili Island. King Uzza landed at Java and slaughtered the last of the Kuru Dynasty. King Uzza made sure his men covered every inch of Indonesia and had everyone pledge to monotheistic belief. He had the people from the other islands brought to Java to be baptized while he and the dragons circled all the islands, looking to see if people were hiding or moving around. The Emperor heard about the siege and sent a letter to King Uzza:

> *About time you got off your butt, and you are doing what*
> *you were placed on this Earth to do. I am proud of you.*
>
> *-The Emperor*

King Uzza burned the letter and had fire in his eyes of hate for his father and brother, King Ibrahim. Time passed, and he took another wife from the Indonesian people to suit his liking; she was named Fitri, meaning purity. The people were terrified of the dragons because they saw the dragons eating people. The people believed the safest place to be in the country was Java, around King Uzza, because he could control the dragons. King Uzza was thinking about what was the next country he could invade where there were pagans. While he was looking at his map of the world he lived in, one of King Uzza's men came in his tent with a letter from Rome's senators.

King Uzza, we heard you've been upset with your father because you are his first-born and heir to the throne more so than your siblings, even though your father does not treat you as his heir of the Emperor's throne and the Dragon Sword. We the people are the voice of Rome. The Senators will give you the Emperor's throne in Rome if you stand with us and take the throne here in Rome.

King Uzza wrote back:

I accept.

CHAPTER 15

King Alexander invaded Spain. The barbarian Celts and other Indo-European tribes put up a fight, but they'd already lost. King Alexander knew he had them outnumbered. He sent in his men, and they killed the rebels, and the people gave up. King Alexander had all them get baptized and took a wife named Ingrid from the Indo-European tribe. She was so beautiful, he married her right away and had his men build her a palace and a sacred house for the people. The tribes liked King Alexander ruling over them; they said he was a just king. Months went by, and King Alexander left his wife, Queen Ingrid conceiving a child and ruling over the people, while he invaded the Philippines. The Negritos people didn't want to die, so they accepted monotheism. They all got baptized, and his men built a sacred house for the monk who was teaching the people the religion. King Alexander left 5,000 soldiers to protect the monks and had them build a castle for the soldiers. He left one of his generals in charge.

The Dragon Emperor heard about the good things King Alexander had done. The Emperor sent his young son, King Yuzhang, on Lava and Hellfire to learn things in Greece. King Yuzhang made it to Greece. King Alexander got on the back of Hellfire, and the dragon went in the air King Alexander couldn't believe he was on the back of a dragon. King Yuzhang told King Alexander he would accompany him on ruling, so he could learn something from him, and the dragon would stay in line. King Alexander laughed and said, "You have grown up fast."

King Yuzhang said, "You have been gone for a while."

King Alexander nodded his head, agreeing with him.

Emperor Quinton had one of the biggest monk schools. All the monks were studying to be monks in Persia, then they were sent out to the people to teach people the monotheism.

Chapter 16

Some time passed, and more kids were born in Emperor Quinton's family. Angel Gabriel came to the Emperor and informed him that the Roman senators had raised an army and hired sorcerers.

"They are plotting to kill their Emperor Diocletian and get your son, King Uzza, to become Emperor and wage war against you with them."

When Emperor Quinton heard the plot against him and the Emperor of Rome, he left to round up his army. Once his army was ready, he took his family with him to make sure they are safe. The Emperor said, "We are going to Rome to move the Roman senators out of power because, for years, it's been nothing but treachery and plotting to overthrow me. Now they are trying to turn my family against me through their wickedness and greed."

His wives and kids were wondering what their father was talking about.

The Emperor informed his friend, General Gaith, to inform his generals, "We are going to Rome to siege Rome and get the senators out of government before they make my son Emperor." The Emperor sent a letter to the senators, informing them he knew of the plot against him. They were thinking there was a trader amongst them. The senators know they could not go to another country because the Emperor had most of the countries under his control.

The senators informed the people of Rome the Dragon Emperor was coming to attack Rome. What the senators didn't know was that Angel Gabriel informed the monks to inform the Roman people that there wouldn't be any harm to them; the Dragon Emperor was coming for the senators. The senators got their paid armies in line, 300,000 Roman soldiers and sorcerers. The Dragon Emperor's ships were covering the Adriatic Sea and the Tyrrhenian Sea; the water dragons were in the air, as well as the ice dragons. He didn't want to burn up the Roman soldiers. The monks informed the people they would not be harmed and to stay indoors. The senators were trying to use the people because they had committed treason. The Emperor on Hyperion, Queen Elizabeth on Waves, King Maximus on Vector, and General Ghaith on Hatuibwari, with Zu Freeze on the side and 200,000 Dragon soldiers in white leather. The Water Dragon Army made it to Rome's battlegrounds to meet the senators with their army. The Emperor told one of his men to give him a horse, and he went out with Genera Gaith and some of his soldiers, and the senators Optimus and Titus came out to talk with the Emperor.

Quinton told the Senator Optimus to, "Inform the senators I am bringing charges of treason for them plotting to overthrow me with the Roman people and my son King Uzza. I know my son despises me because of the success his brothers and sisters, but that's his test with God. He's been failing since the time his brother was been born. In the Biblical times, Jacob's son Joseph went through the same problem with his brothers through all his suffering, and God still gave Joseph a high position in Egypt under the Pharaoh and through all of betrayal from his brothers, he still forgave them and invited all his family to Egypt."

"Since you have your witness to charge me with treason, I want to die here in the field instead of being humiliated and having my head chopped off or being crucified," said Senator Optimus. "This is where you will be judging me according to the monotheistic laws, and I will meet my executor on the battlefield."

The Roman soldiers locked their shields. The Dragon Emperor did something the Roman soldiers had never seen: he pulled his sword off his back. His kids and his men knew how much power the sword possessed. The Roman soldiers let off so many arrows, the sky turned dark, and the Emperor's sword let out fire and disintegrated the arrows. The sorcerers sent tornadoes at the Emperor, but Angel Gabriel pushed the tornadoes up in the air. The sorcerers were wondering how that just happened; the sorcerers made the dragons not see. The dragons landed on the ground, which caused the Emperor sent flames at the sorcerers. The sorcerers disappeared when they reappeared Angel Gabriel's sword cut their heads off. The dragon soldiers and the Roman soldiers were wondering what just happened. The Roman soldiers started to push forward, and the sword extended far enough to cut through the frontline shields. The Emperor's knights and foot soldiers charged.

The war took place with both armies fighting so long, the dirt beneath the battle ground became slippery from the blood spilling from so many dead soldiers. Some of the senators cut their own throat in their tents to not be humiliated and executed in front the Roman people. Once Senator Optimus saw the remaining Roman soldiers retreating, he stabbed himself in the heart. He still was alive, bleeding on the ground. One of the dragon soldiers cut his head off. The Roman Emperor charged into the dragon soldiers and was stabbed by 30 dragon soldiers with daggers, and the rest of the senators were beheaded by the Dragon soldiers. The heads of the senators were placed on display, so the Roman people could see what happened to people when you go against the Dragon Emperor.

For the first time in Roman history, the senators were wiped out, and Rome's government was under one person: the Emperor Maximus and his sister, Queen Elizabeth. Maximus gave Queen Elizabeth Ireland by her being Queen of Scotland to give her quick access to each country since they were connected. Queen Elizabeth told her brother she was standing by him, even if it was against their own brother, King Uzza.

"If he wants what father is giving to you, he going to need to fight for it. God knows what's ahead of us and what's behind us. We just witnessed the work of God on a battlefield when the sorcerer's sent the attack at us that had us lost for words."

The monks took the sword of Emperor's made out of gold and diamonds and passed it from shoulder to shoulder on King Maximus, then he place holy water across on his forehead, then placed the Emperor's crown on his head. King Maximus became Emperor of Rome. The Roman people accepted him without of fear as their ruler. Emperor Quinton got to see his grandson reign.

When King Uzza heard what happened in Rome, he believed his father stole Rome's throne from him. The Emperor sent a letter to his son King Uzza to come in get sworn in as Emperor of India and Indonesia. He wrote his father back, telling him he gave his throne to his brother, King Maximus, and why did he treat him unfair and not like the way he treated Ibrahim and Maximus. The Emperor wrote back I do what God commanded me to do,all y'all my kids you have a great Kingdom and many riches and the bloodline can control dragons and you have dragons how can you be ungrateful I guess this is what God see in you, you want everything because you my first born. King Uzza refuse to come to Rome to get sworn in as Emperor over India and Indonesia. King Ibrahim showed up and was sworn in as Emperor over Norway, Greenland New Zealand and Gual. Emperor Maximus married a descendant of Gaius Julius Caesar, Agrippina, the people of Rome love her when she became empress.

Emperor Maximus married her for her influence over the Roman people, and the fact she was beautiful and had the ambition to rule. She didn't mind Sahara being the First Empress, she being the Second Empress with all three of them sitting on their throne. They gave the Roman people games for 30 days. Emperor Maximus had his whole army keeping eyes on him. When he slept in his chambers, he had a place for his guards in his chambers, special guards at his door, and dragons on his huge balcony, which was built so his dragon could sleep there, keeping people from thinking about coming up. His kids were heavy guarded; all his servants and chefs and gardens and houseworkers were brought from Iceland to attend to him. No Roman citizens were around him except his wife; his father raised him not to trust outside the family.

CHAPTER 17

Scotland Queen Elizabeth made it back to Scotland, she informed her people, "Our kingdom has grown to Ireland."

They started to cheer. Her father by her side, her husband on the other side, the Dragon Emperor said: "This day, I want this nation to know my daughter, Queen Elizabeth is getting sworn in as Empress. The two countries are allies, and she has control over most of the Ice Dragon Army, and she has more ice dragons."

Empress Elizabeth and Emperor Quinton sat down and put the government together for both countries, and General Gaith stayed with her to get her country in order. Empress Elizabeth's army was 300,000 ice dragon soldiers.

The Emperor made it back to Persia. His kids were happy to see him; his wives had a big meal for the family to be together because the Emperor had been away from the family for a while. All through Persia, families were celebrating the conquering of Rome and the family being back from the war. The families lost loved ones, and once everybody was done celebrating for their families coming back home, when the sun went down everybody got together and sent a boat with a candle in it to the sea.

It was time for bed. Quinton the Emperor laid with all his wives, and they were satisfied before they all fell to sleep. God blessed the Emperor to be able to satisfy as many wives of his liking. The Emperor woke up and looked out his window and saw his daughters, Queen Jasmine (12 years old) sword training with her half-sister Suri (12 years old), and both brothers King Saam (11 years old) training with his half-brother Abbas (11 years old). The Emperor was proud seeing his kids getting good with the sword. Once the kids got done training, he told them. The Emperor took them out flying on the fire dragons while the water dragons were in the Persian Gulf hunting for prey.

Once he was done with his journey with the kids, the Emperor arrived back at the palace. His wives, Huayang and Huating, received information that their father was poisoned by their brother, King Qin Er Sh,i because he found out Emperor Qin Shi Huang left his grandkids as his successors. King Qin Er Shi lost his mind and waged war against the Dragon Emperor.

The Emperor hugged his wives and told them, "We've got to kill your brother before he kill us and our kids."

Ships from Persia to China carried 300,000 Fire Dragon soldiers in red leather armor, Death Claw, Smoke, Ryuu, General Gaith on Freeze and Desert Storm. Once the Dragon Army got to China, the Dragon Emperor had a tent set up for his family. Emperor Qin Er Shi didn't waste any time. He sent Godzillas to attack. The Emperor wasn't playing; he cut one of the Godzilla's heads off. Freeze and Desert Storm froze the other Godzilla, then the ice dragons used their tails to shatter him into ice pieces. The two other Godzillas sent flames at the fire dragons, and the fire dragons send their flames at them. The fire dragons were losing the flame battle, so the Emperor cut the first Godzilla's arm and leg off. Once he fell over, the fire dragons' fire overshadowed them, and they were burned up. The Emperor sent the archers to cover the sky with arrows, and the Chinese army shielded the arrows. The fire dragons sent flames at them, disintegrating soldiers while the ice dragons froze the soldiers. The Dragon Army moved in and slaughtered the rest of the Chinese army. Once they brought Qin Er Shi's body to the royal family, they knew they had control of China. China was divided between the grandkids; it was two emperors and two empress, each one of them had 50,000 Dragon soldiers, two water dragons, and two fire dragons.

The Emperor stood in China to oversee the government structure. Wu Zetian was sworn in as Empress of Qin, Su Wu was sworn in as Chu Emperor, Yuzhang is Emperor of Zhao, and Yan and Fu Hao is empress of Wei, Qi and Han. Together, they ruled China.

CHAPTER 18

Quinton the Emperor asked General Gaith where he wanted to be king. He told him once things were together in China, and the Emperor and General Gaith took their family to Jerusalem. Once they got to Jerusalem, they went into the sacred house of Euphrates, and the Emperor informed the monks that General Gaith going to rule over Jerusalem. The monks had the people come together because the Emperor wanted General Gaith to rule Jerusalem and take a Jerusalem wife. The people accepted the Emperor's wishes and the General Gaith was presented five women. General Gaith picked a woman by the name of Hager. She was a woman who spent her life worshiping God and helping with the sick and the poor; she was going to be his Second Queen. General Gaith's wife and his kids accepted him having another wife. The head monk married them, and they laid down for their marriage. The General ordered his men to build her a castle in Judea. It was time for the General to be sworn in as king. General Gaith repeated the words to protect the holy country and the people with his life. When the he finished repeating the words, he was crowned the King of Jerusalem. The people repeated, "Long live King Gaith!"

The Emperor hugged King Gaith and told him to enjoy his retirement. King Gaith just laughed and said, "When you need me, I am there."

"Thank you."

"Do not forget, I have my armor on standby."

The Emperor smiled at him, then he boarded his ship, heading back towards Persia. Once the Emperor got back to Persia, he stood in the secret house, praying to God to grant one of his offspring to bear the Dragon Sword after him. Once he got done praying, he went to his palace. He was accompanied by servants for his bath. His wives were waiting for him in his bed. He laid with the seven of his wives, and they went to sleep satisfied.

The Emperor woke up and saw Saam and Abbas, now 12 years old, sword training with one another. They were moving in the way a father knows: both his sons were going to be great swordsmen. The Emperor took them out hunting deer, and they both caught a deer and were happy. They took the deer home and ate deer and stored the rest.

Great news came to the Emperor. He was having more grandkids. Empress Elizabeth had a daughter name Fiona. Empress Agrippina gave birth to twins, Livilla and Julius. The Emperor and his family left to Rome to see their grandkids. Once he got there, he was so happy looking at his grandkids; he got in instant love for the twins. He picked up one, and empress Delilah picked up the other one. The Roman people were waiting to see the future Emperor .Emperor Maximus held both of his kids up for the Roman people to see and told them it was twin boys. In the Emperor's mind, both kids would rule together, dividing the Roman territory.

Days passed by. It was time to go, but Empress Delilah asked her husband could she stay with her grandkids. The Emperor allow her to. The Emperor started his travel to Scotland. In the palace, he got to see his granddaughter; it was just him and his daughter, Empress Elizabeth. The Emperor held Fiona in his arms when his daughter asked him, had he seen Uzza? The Emperor told her, "Your brother has wickedness in his heart towards his brothers and sisters, and he is going to bring total destruction into our family. Nobody can change it except him. God is testing him, and he is failing. He is too in tune into this life and not worrying about the hereafter. I am leaving it in God's hands. No matter what, the outcome comes, but as long as I'm alive, the first one of my kids who sheds their own brother or sister's blood, I will raise war on them. When I am gone, it's out my hands."

Empress Elizabeth understood what her father was saying and told her father she would keep fighting for what was right according to monotheistic laws. The Emperor informed his daughter her mother was staying in Rome, so she should expect her coming this way soon.

"That's great! When she comes here, I am going hold her hostage with me."

The Emperor started to laugh.

The Emperor stayed in Scotland for a couple days, then went off to Norway to see his son, Emperor Ibrahim. Emperor Ibrahim was lost with words when his men inform him the Emperor of Emperors and the royal family was approaching the kingdom. All you saw was 10,000 Fire Dragon soldiers in red leather armor and Death Claw and Smoke behind her. Ryuu was back, protecting the Kingdom of Persia.

As the royal family was entering the palace, the Ice Dragons soldiers were kneeling down. The Emperor Ibrahim was happy and surprised to see his family. His mother, Empress Abijah, smiled at him. Emperor Ibrahim came to his mother and bowed down and kissed her hand. She picked him up and hugged him. The grandkids saw their grandmother and came to her and gave her hugs and kisses. The Emperor Ibrahim had the servants prepare food for the royal family.

They sat, ate, and laughed. Days went by, and in the night, Angel Azrael came to Quinton and informed him he was the Angel of Death. Quinton asked him is it was his time. The Angel of Death said, "Not yet. I am here because you have one more war to fight for God, and it's against half-angel and half-man. They are call 'Nephilims,' and they rebel against God. The Nephilims are powerful and have bow and arrows made out of light that can kill dragons and angels. Spears big like harpoons made out of light that can kill dragons. The advantage is, you have all dragons of all the elements that you must fight them with. Some dragons are going to die; some of your men are going to die, but you will prevail by wiping all of them out and not leaving any of them alive. This is your commandment. The place of the Nephilims is in Canaan, which is in your kingdom. They are planning to have more Nephilims on Earth to enslave the human civilization."

The morning hours struck the Emperor of Emperors.

"Inform Emperor Ibrahim we have a war on our hands that man cannot fight. Our armies will get slaughtered. The Nephilims, they are very powerful, and their weapons are made out of light and can kill dragons and angels if they are struck by them. If we do not fight this war, the Nephilims will breed with more humans and put men into slavery, and we will have disobeyed God's commandment. The Nephilims want to build an army to take over the world and curse God. We need Blizzard, Snowfall, Cloud, Naga, and Frost Storm. I am leaving your mother here; it's safe for her here."

The Emperor sent both his wives, Huating and Huayang, to China to be with their kids and be safe there. Both his wives Nadia and Soraya came with him, and his son, Emperor Ibrahim, while heading back to Persia. The Emperor told Ibrahim, "We have conquered the world and fought for the cause of God with His power and guidance. I will soon leave you and your brothers and sisters. I want you to always do what God commands you to do."

"I will, Father," Ibrahim said, worrying about his father.

Once they got to Persia, the Emperor told his wives and kids to go into the palace.

The Emperor raised the sword to the sky, all the dragons turned to the empresses and emperors and told them, "The Dragon Emperor summoned us." All the Emperor kids were forced to come with all the dragons to Persia. Once they got to Persia, the Emperor words, the Emperor told them, "I summoned it the dragons here because we are at war with a great power that lies ahead that could cause human life to be extinct. I was given orders by God to stop the Nephilims, which are half-angels and half-man and have power of angels and weapons that can kill dragons and angels. I want my kids to stay here because this war maybe my last one. The Angels of death told me."

As the Emperor was leaving with all the dragons, Ibrahim got on Smoke to follow behind his father.

Canaan housed over 200 Nephilims and dwarfs as their slave workers. The Nephilims start shooting arrows once they saw the dragons, and God sent his soldiers, angels Michael and Gabriel, to help with the fight. From the air, the fire dragons were sending flames down on the Nephilims and disintegrated them; the ice dragons froze the Nephilims and used their tails to shatter them into ice pieces; the water dragons knocked them down. The Dragon Emperor got off Death Claw to fight side by side with Angel Michael and Angel Gabriel. The Dragon Emperor was cutting the Nephilims in half and setting them on fire, and freezing the Nephilims and cutting them up in big, ice pieces of meat. The Nephilims' arrows hit Lava as Lava came down on some of the giant Nephilims and killed two of Nephilims before he died. Waves and Vector were hit by spears and arrows in their hearts, but as they were going down, they fell on a Nephilim, killing one of them. The Dragon Emperor, Angel Michael, and Angel Gabriel were cutting the Nephilims to their death. The dwarfs were sending balls of fire at the dragons.

The fire dragons were disintegrating the giant Nephilims while the ice dragons were freezing them; the water dragons were knocking them down but not killing them because they were too strong to die from the water dragons' force. Hellfire was riddled with arrows, but as he was going down, he killed three Nephilims. Death Claws, Ryuu, and Smoke were sending flames like no other fire dragons, killing the Nephilims and the dwarfs. Every time the giant Nephilims sent arrows, spears, and swung their swords at Death Claw, Ryuu, and Smoke, they were missing. Stormbreaker and Frozen were shot out of the air with arrows and cut in pieces. The Dragon Emperor killed the Nephilims who killed Stormbreaker and Frozen. Zu, Vipor, Haku, Blaze were hurt.

As the Nephilims were almost all killed, one of the Nephilims fell, causing the Dragon Emperor to be injured. Angel Michael, Angel Gabriel Death Claw, Smoke, and Ryuu protected the Dragon Emperor while Sandstorm, Dragor, and Snake Eyes killed the last of the Nephilims and the dwarfs.

Once the war was over, Canaan was destroyed by the dragons and the Angels. The Dragon Emperor woke up with his back broken and bleeding to the brain. He was being carried back to the palace on a horse and carriage with the sword on his chest placed there by Angel Michael. The Emperor was placed in his bed while his family was looking over him helpless. King Uzza was thinking about if he was going to be the one bear the Sword.

Days went by, and the Emperor of Emperors was in a coma state. God gave him more time to set his family straight. Late that day, the Emperor woke up, and standing over him was Emperor Ibrahim and Empress Elizabeth. The Emperor smiled at them and said, "God gave me more time to get the family in order. Call your brothers and sisters in here. I know the family realizes I am not going to be able to walk again. We lost Lava, Hellfire Frozen, Stormbreaker, Waves, and Vector, and others got injured like me. The dragons are going to go where I send them and to whom I send them."

King Uzza left out the room and made a statement, "If you had died, we could have done what we wanted to do."

"May God have mercy on your soul," the Emperor said.

As King Uzza was leaving upset, he passed his little brothers Saam and Abbas and asked them what they were looking at, then King Uzza pull them. Abbas fell, and the both of them were upset. Abbas got up and continued proceeding to his father's chambers with the rest of the siblings. Abbas and Saam accompanied their father.

"Call my head generals in here."

General Sual entered the chambers.

"Yes Emperor of Emperors?"

"How are the dragons?"

"They are recovering."

"I want you to bring me the list of names of all the dragons that are in the dungeons beneath the palace and the water dragons out in the sea." The General brought him the list. The Emperor decided where the dragons were going from his list. Egypt would have Blaze and Vipor; Africa, Malinda and Rhaegal; Rome, Sandstorm, Hellos, and Hail; Iceland, Blizzard, Eingana, Cloud, and Zu. For Babylon's future, Ryuu, Hydro, and Hyperion; Norway would have Freeze, Desert, and Naga; Persia would keep Death Claw, Nyres, Neutral, and Smoke. China would keep Snake Eyes, Dragor, Haku, and Rainstorm, and India would have Egan, Hatuibwari, and Desert Storm.

Once the Emperor was done dictating where the dragons were going, he summoned for his craftsman to design him a comfortable chair with wheels, so he could get around. The craftsman worked days and nights to get the chair with wheels ready, so his Emperor could get around. Once he was done with the chair on wheels, he immediately bought it to the Emperor, and the Emperor loved what he built for him and order his men to give the craftsman a small pouch of gold. The craftsman left, satisfied.

For the first time in weeks, the Emperor was outside. While outside, the Emperor raised his sword and made the sword go through the elements, then he summoned the dragons to him. All the dragons came to him; the people of Persia knew the Emperor was summoning the dragons to him. Each one of the Emperor's kids took their dragons and went back to their kingdoms.

The Emperor informed his men to build Babylon back up for his son Saam to rule. The remaining water dragons went back to the Mediterranean Sea, and the fire dragons tried to get the Emperor up out of his seat. His men put him on Death Claw, and the Emperor was flying around with joy in his heart, like when he was a kid on Death Claw. Hours went by, and the Emperor came back home. His men got him off Death Claw and took him back into the palace. The Emperor had supper with his family.

The Emperor spent the next six years building Babylon and a resting place in the palace for the Dragon Sword. He visited all the people over the world, giving them ceremonies of the true God of Abraham until, one day, he didn't wake up in his bed. The Angel of death finally slipped his soul out of his body, gently. His wives discovered he was no longer with the world and his family.

Angel Gabriel placed the sword into the stone in the sacred house. People from all around the world heard about the Emperor of Emperors passing away and came to visit the Emperor to see if it was true. The viewing was in the sacred house, and it lasted for two days. The Emperor was placed under his palace in a marble casket with silk inside and a see-through top, and his crown was on his head. He held a replica of the Dragon Sword in his hands. The sword was placed in the sacred house, where every man tried to take the sword out of the stone, and some men tried to chisel it out. Many times, they failed. The monks live with the Dragon Sword.

The Emperor's son, King Uzza, came to his father's gravesite in the palace.

"I am glad you are dead. I've grown to hate you for not making me your successor. I was your first-born. Every king and every great ruler's first-born was his successor. You could have talked to God to allow me to bear the sword."

Emperor Abbas was in the walls of the palace. He heard his brother talking to his father.

"Now you are gone, I am going to wage war against all my brothers and sisters until they are all dead, and I am the last one standing to be able to bear the Dragon Sword and rule the world."

He kissed his father, turned, and said, "So long, Father."

King Uzza left the palace and went back to India. Emperor Abbas explained what he just heard to Saam, Maximus, Elizabeth, Wu Zetian, Su Wu. Then once he explained what he just heard, he told them, "Do not tell anybody else. We need to make sure his mother's kids aren't with him."

They all agreed. They feasted, sang, and slept in the chambers where their father's body laid. A month passed, and the plot begin. King Uzza went to his mother kids to ask them to join him to wage war on his brothers and sisters from different mothers, to divide the kingdom with the four oldest of Emperor Quinton. Everyone agreed except Emperor Ibrahim. Empress Yara and her army in white leather armor met King Uzza with her army in India. Accompanying him was Empress Khadijah with her army, also in white leather armor. King Uzza's army was in black leather armor. They marched their army to China.

King Uzza, Empress Yara, and Empress Khadijah met with their half-brothers Su Wu and Yuzhang and half-sisters Fu Hao and Wu Zatien. Standing behind them was their army in red leather. King Uzza spoke, "My mother's kids are the rightful rulers of the world. We are the oldest of our father's kids. Bow down to us, and we will let you live."

"You know what's funny, we knew you were coming, and we know your last words to our father when you were standing over his casket. Were you going to kill all us to be the last one standing to bear the sword? Abbas was between the walls, hearing you talk to our father," Su Wu said.

"These are lies."

"We all know, Uzza. The other ones who didn't know are your mother kids, because we didn't trust them."

Yara and Khadijah look at him and said, "Is this true?"

"No, we have the same mother. I would never take your life. For the last time, bow down to us."

"Over our dead bodies."

They all went back to their place on the front line and started giving orders. Archers on both sides started throwing arrows. Both armies put up their shields, but soldiers still died. Both armies sent out knights. They knocked one another down; the foot soldiers pushed forward and crashed into each other. They fought until they were weak, and hundreds of thousands of people were dead. The dragons then attacked one another: Blaze, Vipor, Malinda, Rhaegal, Egan, Hatuibwari, and Desert Storm attacked. Snake Eyes, Dragor, Haku, and Rainstorm were hit from all sides, killing three dragons, and Su Wu, Wu Zetian, Fu Hao died also. Yuzhang fell off Dragor and hit the ground. Dragor lived because he got hit from the water dragon pressure, pushing him back, and Yuzhang fall off Dragor, hitting the ground and breaking both legs then getting knocked unconscious. King Uzza thought his brother Yuzhang died also and took Dragor to make his attack stronger against his brothers and sisters. The remaining soldiers found Su Wu, Wu Zetian, and Fu Hao dead, and Yuzhang alive but badly injured.

The Emperor and Empresses' bodies were place in marble caskets inside with see-through tops and mummified from the damages of their corpse. Emperor Yuzhang was on bed, rest getting medical treatment.

King Uzza invaded Greece, slaughtering King Alexander's men, looking for King Alexander. When he couldn't find him, he turned to his soldiers to submit to him, and the soldiers bowed down to King Uzza. King Alexander escaped to Jerusalem to warned King Gaith about King Uzza's plot. King Alexander explained what was going on, and King Gaith and King Alexander, accompanied by a group of men, left to Persia to warn Emperor Abbas what was going on. King Uzza got to Jerusalem and found out King Gaith wasn't there. He tortured some of King Gaith's men to death, trying to find out where King Gaith and King Alexander were. Once he came to the terms they did not know where King Gaith and King Alexander were, he had some of the soldiers join him.

Two days passed, and King Gaith and King Alexander made it to Persia. They immediately informed the Emperor of Persia. The Emperor of Persia had his best men go take three water dragons to go to Rome, Norway, and Iceland to get the message to his brothers and sisters. The Emperor and his brother, Saam, were already waiting for this day.

The Emperor had over 100,000 soldiers waiting by the Mediterranean Sea and Abbas on Death Claw, King Gaith on Smoke, Emperor Saam on Ryuu, and King Alexander on Hydro. They had tents up, waiting to see if they saw the ships and men. Emperor Abbas informed them, "We're going straight for the heart and killing King Uzza."

They all agreed. The four of them met up with Emperor Ibrahim first and his sons King Gaius and King Azam, and Empress Elizabeth and Emperor Maximus.

They all were heading back to Persia. Once they got there, King Uzza was slaughtering Emperor Abbas's men. Emperor Abbas's soldiers were holding the dragons back. Many stations were set up sending harpoons at the dragons, killing Rainstorm and leaving King Uzza with seven dragons. Emperor Ibrahim told his kids to get off the dragons and go to the sacred house with the monks. Emperor Ibrahim went to attack his brother King Uzza on Egan. He sent flames at Emperor Ibrahim; the ice dragon breaths were no match, killing Ibrahim, Freeze and Desert. Death Claw and Smoke sent flames at Egan, killing Egan and King Uzza. Empress Yara kill two of the water dragons, Nyres and Haku. Death Claw and Smoke sent flames on Malinda and Empress Yara, killing her and Malinda. The soldiers fighting from the ships, half of King Uzza's men made it on dry land. Emperor Abbas's Dragon soldiers were out numbering King Uzza's Dragon soldiers on land. In the sacred house, Azam was praying to God to stop the bloodshed between brothers and sisters

Emperor Khadijah killed Hatuibwari and Desert Storm. A whisper from Angel Gabriel came to King Azam: "You are the Chosen One."

He got up like he was possessed and walked to the sword. The sword lit up when he got near the sword. King Azam took both hands and pulled the sword out of the stone with both hands. The sky lit up; also the Dragon soldiers and the dragons stopped fighting. All the dragons knew there was another Emperor bearing the sword. The dragons stopped fighting and fell to the ground, waiting to see who was bearing the sword to submit.

The war stopped. The soldiers put down their weapons, and King Azam came out with the Dragon Sword and put the sword in the air.

"Hear my words: I speak for my forefather, Emperor or Emperors. I am the Chosen One to bear the Dragon Sword. I am the Emperor of Emperors over the dragons; emperors, empresses, and Dragon soldiers; kings and the inhabitants of the world. We have failed our God by killing one another over greed, arrogance, and pridefulness. You have failed the test I've been warning you about all this time. I ask my creator, God Almighty, to forgive y'all. Now, you must get on your knees and ask God Almighty for forgiveness and mean it in your heart. God knows the heart of the deceiver and of the ones who tell the truth. Farewell, my children, know I am waiting for y'all in heaven with God."

Emperor Azam fell over once he was done talking. The power from above took over his body, and once Emperor Quinton left his body, that made him weak enough to fall over. The dragons stood by the Emperor Azam. Emperor Azam became conscious and got up.

"As me, your Emperor of Emperors, I order the brothers and sisters to purify themselves through baptism."

They all got baptized again. Then, the Emperor gave Egypt, Rhaegal, and Rome, Dragor. Norway, Death Claw and Naga. India, Blaze. Africa, Sandstorm. Iceland, Blizzard and Eingana. Babylon, Ryuu and Zu. Persia, Smoke and Cloud. China, Hail. Jerusalem, Hydro, and Greece, Hyperion. Then the Emperor went around the world visiting people and learning the dragon power of the sword.